Donnie opened the door to his bedroom and saw a surprise. On his bed was a BIG box wrapped in paper with a bow on it.

1

He ran to the kitchen to find his
mother, so he could ask what
she knew about the big box.

Mary, Donnie's mother, told him
it was a birthday gift from
Donnie's Uncle Neal. "Go ahead
and open it," she said.

Donnie ripped off the paper and saw that the box contained building blocks, something he always wanted!

Donnie couldn't wait to take out
the blocks and start using
his wild imagination to build
amazing things.

Mary told Donnie that before he started playing with the blocks, he had to write a thank you note. It would go to Uncle Neal to express his gratitude for the gift.

"What is gratitude?" Donnie
asked his mother.

Mary answered, "It's giving
thanks for something you
receive. The more grateful you
are, the more you will receive.
We should go to sleep and
wake up being grateful."

"The perfect way to express your gratitude is by writing a thank you note," she added as she took a note card out of a box.

They sat down to write a note.

Dear Uncle Neal,

Thank you for the gift of building blocks. I will think of you when I play with them.

With love and gratitude,

Donnie

Donnie put the note in an envelope and ran outside to put the card in the mailbox.

Then Donnie decided to run to the edge of the forest where he loved to sit and watch his animal friends.

He noticed one deer bringing a branch with berries on it and laying it down in front of another deer.

The deer rubbed his nose up against the deer that brought the gift of berries.

Donnie also saw a squirrel
bringing another squirrel an
acorn and placing it in front of
him.

15

The squirrel that got the acorn came close and gave a kiss to the other squirrel.

Donnie had an idea!! He walked
around the forest picking fruit
and nuts that were on the trees.

He placed the food on the
ground at the edge of the forest.
He sat down to wait.

It wasn't long before two deer
and some squirrels slowly
walked up to Donnie.

At that point the animals began
to eat the fruit and nuts.

One deer using his nose pushed
an apple towards Donnie.
Donnie began to smile.

He ran back to the house with
the apple and found his mother
in the kitchen.

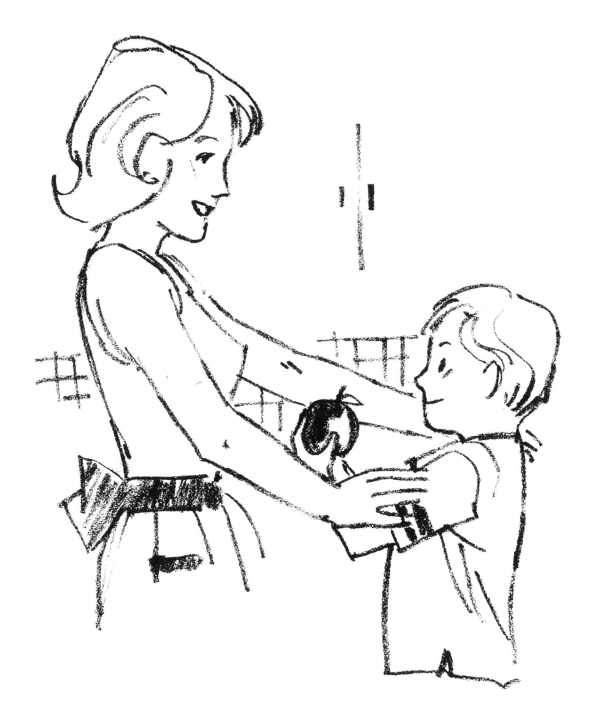

Donnie told his mother what he
saw the animals do in the forest.

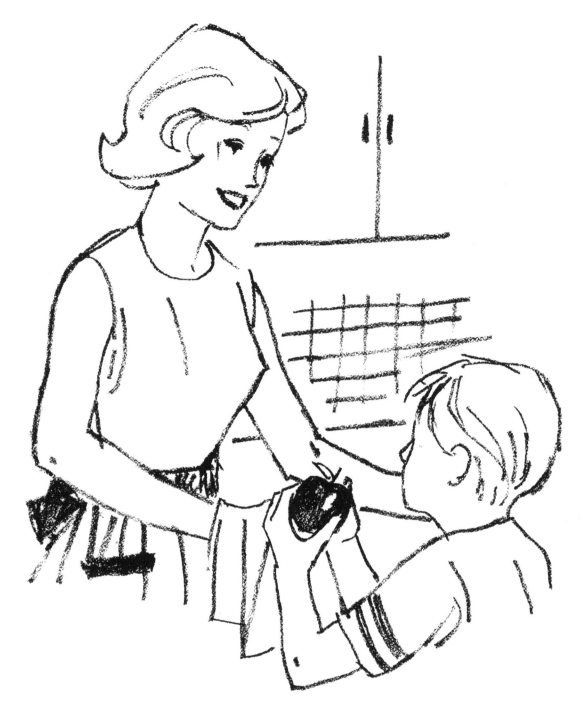

Mary said, "That's exactly what gratitude is about, you can show thanks in many different ways."

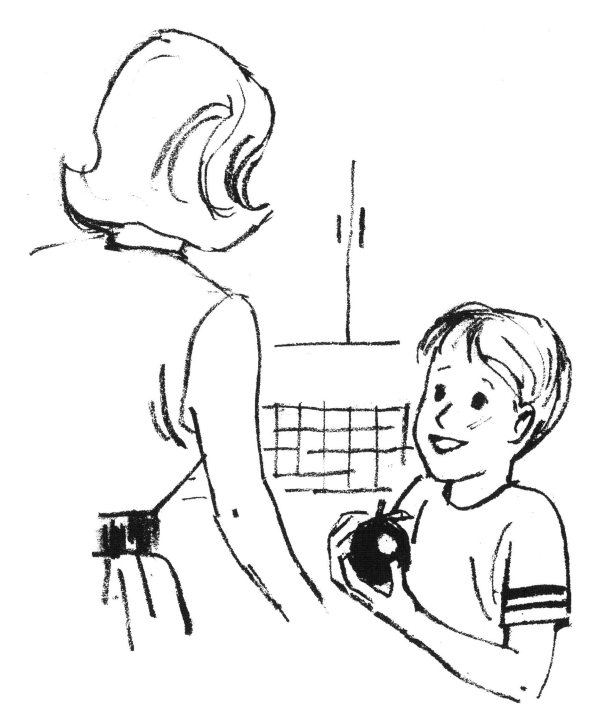

"Do you think I should write a thank you note to the animals for my apple?" Donnie asked.

"People write thank you notes to the person who gives them the gift. If you feel like writing one, go ahead," Mary said with a smile.

26

Donnie took out a card and

begin to write:

Dear Animal Friends,

Thank you for the apple. I will

eat it for my snack today.

With love,

Donnie

27

Donnie ran out to the edge of
the forest and put the card
down on the ground. He placed
it where he usually sits.

Suddenly Donnie heard his mom calling him, "You have a phone call!"

Donnie ran into the kitchen. His mother handed him the phone.

"Hi Donnie, this is Uncle Neal.
I just received the beautiful
thank you note you wrote.
I really appreciated it. Now I
have an idea of what to get you
for the holidays."

"WOW, really Uncle Neal? I can't believe it," exclaimed Donnie.

"Well it's true! The more you show your gratitude, the more you will receive. I wish more children would learn the value of writing *Thank You* notes. I love you. Bye bye."

Blank Thank You Notes

From

To

From

To

From

To

From

To

46069018R00040